Porridge the
Tartan Cat

For my neighbours, Dawn and Michael,
and their big brawsome family – A.D.

For my cat Frankie –
the opposite of Porridge, but still... – Y.S.

Kelpies is an imprint of Floris Books
First published in 2017 by Floris Books
Text © 2017 Alan Dapré. Illustrations © 2017 Floris Books
Alan Dapré and Yuliya Somina have asserted their rights
under the Copyright, Designs and Patent Act 1988 to
be identified as the Author and Illustrator of this work

The publisher acknowledges subsidy from
Creative Scotland towards the publication
of this volume

FSC
www.fsc.org
MIX
Paper from
responsible sources
FSC® C117931

e  Also available as an eBook

British Library CIP data available
ISBN 978-178250-358-3
Printed & bound by MBM Print SCS Ltd, Glasgow

# Porridge the Tartan Cat and the Loch Ness Mess

Written by Alan Dapré

Illustrated by Yuliya Somina

Young Kelpies

THIS BRAW BOOK BELONGS TO

## Porridge the Tartan Cat

Scratch my ears and
you can read it too.

# 1

# Su-purr Porridge

Hi, I'm Porridge the Tartan Cat.

I'd love to know your name.

Write it on the dotted line below.

THIS IS TO CERTIFY THAT THIS BOOK IS THE BEST BOOK I'VE EVER READ (EVEN THOUGH I HAVEN'T READ IT YET).

SIGNED ........................................................

I live in Tattiebogle town with Ross and Isla, the McFun twins. We all go on incredible adventures together. Afterwards, I cat-a-log each tartan ~~tail~~ tale into a fabuliffic book just like this one.

*Porridge the Tartan Cat and the Loch Ness Mess* is packed with Porridge. (Me, not the gloopy stuff you have for breakfast.) And it's all about a famous loch, full of mystery... and fish.

## Mmmm. Fish.

Why not make yourself comfortable and enjoy a magical adventure where wishes really do come true?

## Me-wow!

# 2

# Heads or Heads

## FLUBB~LUBB~A~LUBB~LUB~LUB!

That was the sound the washing machine made as it flubb-lubb-a-lubb-lub-lubbed to a stop. The McFun twins watched their dad open the round door and take out my tartan blanket. It had shrunk to the size of this wee page.

 **Me-sigh**

"You need to follow the instructions," said Ross.

Aye, Dad had washed it on the *I've-no-idea-what-this-button-does-but-I'll-press-it-anyway* setting!

"Sorry about that, Porridge," he said, with a shrug. "These new machines have too many fiddly buttons and instructions. I like really old things, like really old fossils."

"And really old jokes," giggled Isla.

"Here's a good one," said Dad, dusting off his favourite joke. "What do you call a dinosaur with no eyes?"

# 3... 2... 1...

"A dnosaur!"

Ross groaned. "That joke is so old I bet the dinosaurs invented it."

"Want to see something else really old?" Dad showed the twins a dusty coin. "I found this Roman denarius on Hadrian's Wall."

"Well, on *my* wall I've got a poster of Hamish

McBoot," giggled Isla. "He's playing in the Cup Final today. Can we watch the match?"

"I'd rather you two came out on a fossil hunt with me – it's a lovely day for digging!" Dad gazed at the sunny sky full of sun and, er, sky. "Here's what we'll do. I'll toss this coin and if it lands on TAILS you can stay in and see the match, but if it's HEADS you're both coming to Loch Ness with me. I have a feeling in my bones we'll find some dinosaur bones. Long ago, dinosaurs walked around Scotland!"

*Only because cars weren't invented*, I meowed.

"What's that, Porridge?" said Isla.

"I think he wants to come too," said Ross.

"Only if it's HEADS." Dad flicked the coin so high it nearly flew off the page. It tinkled to a stop by my furry front paws. "HEADS!" he said, without looking.

The twins peered down at the head of an old Roman emperor.

"Dad wins," said Isla.

"I guess we need to get ready," said Ross.

They trudged into the hallway to get their coats. I was already wearing my fur coat so I stayed put. Dad reached down for the denarius, but before he could touch it, I flipped it over with a suspicious claw. Both sides were HEADS!

## 🐾 Me-trick! 🐾

"It's a double-headed coin," said Dad, winking at me. He pocketed the coin and picked up a dusty bag of tools for the impending dig. "You'll love this, Porridge. Digging is fun."

*Aye, for daft dugs.*

I padded towards the car behind Dad and the twins. The air was full of strange chomping sounds and not-so-strange grass clippings. Mum and Gran were in the front garden with Gadget Grandad, trying out his GrassGnasher.

"I made it out of old false teeth," explained Grandad, with a toothy grin.

## 🐾 Me-chomp! 🐾

"By gum, it nibbles the grass super-short," cried Mum, who liked super-short things (especially shortbread).

"Porridge! Watch out for ma wallies!" warned Gran,

as the gnawing gnashers nearly nipped ma tail.

I scarpered straight into the car and curled in a cosy

cat box, beside the twins.

"Time to go to Loch Ness and find some fossils!"

said Dad, keen to turn the key and start the car.

*Time to go to Loch Ness and find some fish!* meowed

me, keen to turn the page and start the next chapter...

# 3

# The Next Chapter

By the magic of storytelling, we arrived at Loch Ness quicker than you can say, "It's not really magic, it's just turning a page."

Ahead of us was a wide stretch of cold wet water.

 **Me-brrr** 🐾

And a grey, stony beach that looked like a big cat litter tray. At one end, we saw an unusual sight. A rusty old helicopter was getting ready to take off. The wind from its chop-chop-choppy blades made the water chop-chop-choppy too.

*I guess that's why it's called a chopper.*

An eager line of tourists climbed aboard, wearing
t-shirts that said:

The blades whirled faster and the chopper lifted
off. It rattled and clattered over my head, and the
passengers took pictures of a cool tartan cat.

(Me, of course.)

"Will the tourists find Nessie?" asked Isla, as the chopper flew over the mysterious grey water.

"That's impossible," said Dad. "But *we* might find dinosaur bones under our feet."

*Hmmm. While they're looking for a legend, we might find a leg end!*

(A legend always has a grain of truth in it – especially The Legend of the Grain of Truth. *I* think the Loch Ness Monster is as real as you and me. Och, as real as me anyway, I'm not sure about you.)

Dino Dad led us to a patch of dusty ground that had been roped off so archaeologists like him could dig for bones. I padded towards the nearby loch, hoping to find a wee school of fish – *or a big university of fish*.

## 🐾 Me-yum! 🐾

The view was brawsome. Ross and Isla came to look with me.

"That waterfall over there is like a white curtain," said Isla, with a lovely smile. (And a lovely simile.)

"I'd love to see a monster, especially Nessie."

"How about a monster footprint? Here's one." Dad knelt by a deep dent in the ground. "It was made millions of years ago by a dinosaur."

"What made *that* footprint?" Isla pointed to some wet prints by the shore.

"A soggy tartan cat," chuckled Dad.

 **Me-drip** 

(NEVER try to get fish from a loch. Always get them from a fishmonger. That's my top tartan tip.)

I sat on a comfy mound of earth and dried my wet fur in the warm sunshine. I swept my tail happily from side to side, whipping up dust that tickled my nose.

Words blew everywhere like the dust. It took me ages to find them all.

 **Me-oops**

Everyone else was busy. The twins were busy sweeping away the soil looking for dino bones. Dad was busy scribbling notes. And I was busy sitting on ma bahookie. (It's a cat thing.)

## 🐾 Me-yawn 🐾

"Have you found anything?" I heard Dad ask the twins.

"One rusty nail," replied Isla.

"Two dusty snails," added Ross, placing them under a shady bush.

I was feeling hot so I stylishly swished my tail again, because it keeps me cool. (And looks cool too).

Dad spied something under my tail. Suddenly, his eyes lit up like two candles on a toddler's cake. He did a daft dance like a dad at a disco. "Congratulations, Porridge. You've found a big bone!"

#  Me-what!? 

*Don't tell anyone. Especially not a daft dug.*

##  Me-cringe

Ross and Isla helped Dad dig away more of the mud. They gazed in wonder at a huge, Y-shaped bone.

"What is it, Dad?" asked Isla.

"A spellbinding discovery," said the excited archaeologist. He spun on his heels then froze on one leg and had a wee think for the rest of this sentence. "I think it's a fossilised furcula: in other words, a big old wishbone."

"Is it from a giant chicken?" joked Ross.

"A mighty megalosaurus, more like," gushed Dad. "It's my favourite dinosaur."

He gave the wishbone a really big **HUG**.

At once the air crackled and the wishbone glowed, but Dad didn't seem to notice. Next, to pull it out of the ground, he gave it really big **TUG**!

And *that* was when the trouble began...

# MIGHTY-MEGA TROUBLE!

## 🐾 Me-oops! 🐾

# 4

# The Wish

"I love megalosauruses. I wish *I* was a mighty megalosaurus," said Dad, just as the massive magical wishbone went

**SNAP!**

And in a mighty-mega

**FLASH**

his wish came true!

 **Me-wow!**

He grew mighty-mega claws and mighty-mega jaws, mighty-mega scales and a mighty-mega tail! It was a sight that I'll *never* forget. (Och, if I do forget, I'll read this chapter again.)

Everything about the megalosaurus was mighty-mega, and if I have to write mighty-mega any more I'll get grumpy.

*Mighty-mega grrrumpy.*

"It's megamazincredibrill..." spluttered Ross.

"It's Dino Dad!" yelled Isla.

Dino Dad gazed at his reflection in the silvery water, then roared with delight! The twins couldn't believe their eyes. So I grabbed Dad's phone out of his bag and took a quick selfie with the dinosaur in the background doing a daft Dino Dad dance.

## 🐾 Me-selfie! 🐾

(I'll show it to you later, if you like.)

I put the phone back and gawped at Dino Dad.

Dino Dad scooped up the twins in his claws and spun them around playfully. He twirled them in circles like a roundabout. Then rocked them up and down like a dino-see-saw.

"This is ultramazincredibrilliant!" whooped Ross.

"*Way* better than the play park," shouted Isla, sliding down Dino Dad's tail.

"I love having a Dino Dad," giggled Ross.

"Me too," agreed Isla. "The trouble is, he's too big to drive us home, or fit in our house."

"You're right," replied Ross, frowning a little.

"We're going to have to change him back somehow," said his sister.

Dino Dad ran past them, looking hot and bothered from all the spinning.

"We'll have to catch him first!" said Ross.

Dino Dad leapt into the loch to cool off.

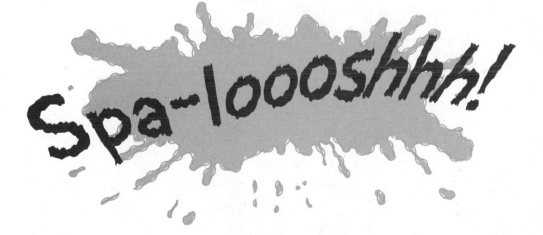

Water went everywhere! And I mean
EVERYWHERE! So this book might be a bit soggy
round the edges (like me). Sorry about that.

🐾 **Me-drip** 🐾

# 5
# Fun Guy

## CHOP-CHOP-CHOP

The twirling, swirling, Nessie-hunting helicopter was heading back to the shore! Eager tourists snapped Dino Dad with their mighty megapixel cameras.

SNAP SNAP SNAP

And Dino Dad snapped back with his mighty-mega pointy jaws.

SNAP SNAP SNAP

The helicopter **buzzed** around Dino Dad like a pesky fly. Then it swooped down low, landed, and six dizzy tourists tumbled onto the shore. The grinning pilot stepped out and shooed them away. Then he turned to stare at us.

 Me-gulp!

I had spotted a spotted toadstool on his captain's hat. The twins did too.

"There's only one guy *that* fond of fungi," gasped Ross.

The three of us shouted out his name (if you know it, join in too):

# FERGUS MCFUNGUS!

Maybe you recognise him from another of my adventures? He is mouldier than a mushy mushroom, and rotten as a zombie's teeth. All he ever wants to do is take over the world... and destroy things like volcanoes and fishy biscuits and elephants.

 **Me-groan** 🐾

# "AT LAST I'VE FOUND THE LOCH NESS MONSTER!"

said Fergus, with great big sighs of relief and, um, great big letters of relief too.

"It's NOT Nessie!" yelled Isla.

"And it's NOT a monster!" cried Ross. "It's our dad and he's really nice. He reads us stories at night *and* lets us stay up late at the weekend."

Fergus didn't believe them. "This big beastie has terrible jaws, cruel claws and evil elbows. It looks like a monster to me! Soon it will be mine, all mine. Mwah-ha-ha!"

"Why?" asked Isla.

"Because I'm a master criminal who is up to no good," boasted Fergus, "and here's ma signed certificate to prove it!" He held up something shiny.

"That's a crisp packet!" groaned Ross. "You just scoffed all the crisps and wrote your name on it."

Fergus groaned back. "OK, I *don't* have a certificate but I *do* have a MONSTROUS plan. A plan so monstrous it must be muttered very quietly so no meddling kids can hear. First, I'll fly this MONSTER to ma secret secret ship out at sea. Then I'll scan and 3D-print it and create an ARMY of MONSTERS so I can take over the world and destroy all the volcanoes and fishy biscuits and, um, the other thing..."

*Elephants.*

"You're rubbish at muttering, Fergus," said Isla. "We heard all of your plan."

"Bah. I'm much better at snatching monsters!" With that, Fergus hopped into his helicopter, flew up high and hovered right over Dino Dad's head. He opened a hatch and lowered a giant grabber – as if he was trying to win a teddy from a toy machine!

# NOOOOO!

I wailed.

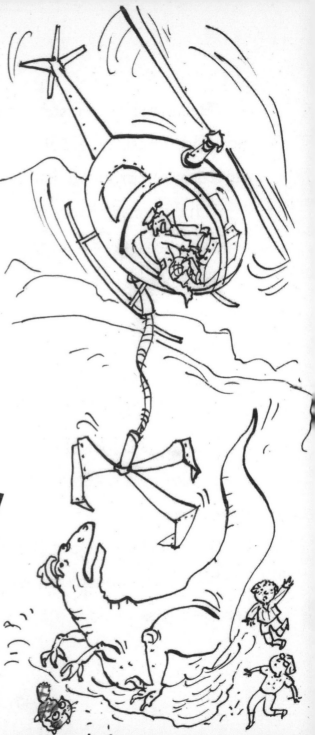

The twins wailed too. "Leave our Dino Dad alone!"

All at once, the grabber's three metal fingers closed with a colossal

# CLANG!

and missed Dino Dad by the thickness of this page!

🐾 Me-phew! 🐾

"Bah, this is just like the time I tried to pick up a toy teddy!" grumbled Fergus, lifting the grabber to have another go.

"Run!" cried Isla, but Dino Dad didn't budge.

"Maybe he doesn't understand humans any more," groaned Ross.

"What about clever cats?" Isla looked at me with hope in her eyes and a fishy biscuit in her fingers.

*It was worth a try.* As you know, I speak lots of languages, except Mouse. (Actually, I squeak that.)

"Run and hide!" I ordered, in a croaky, rasping hiss.

*Och, I spoke Dinosaur!*

Dino Dad nodded slowly then started to run.

"Nice one, Porridge," said Isla, handing over a wee fishy treat.

## 🐾 Me-yum 🐾

Dino Dad stepped over a wooden gate and lumbered across a crowded campsite.

"Follow that dinosaur," shouted Ross. It wasn't easy. I had to squ-eeeeeeeee-ze under the gate, tear across a field full of tents. *And <u>not</u> trip on any*

*pesky tent ropes.*

# 6

# I'm OK!

I tumbled on the grass and skidded to a full stop by this comma, which was a bit confusing. Punctuation is like that.

To my surprise, I saw a friendly face that belonged to a big pal of mine. And a friendly trunk that belonged to a big pal of mine. And friendly legs that belonged to a big pal of mine. And a friendly belly... and a friendly bahookie... and two friendly ears... *And* if you put all that together you get Basil the friendly elephant, a *big* pal of mine!

Basil was on holiday with his owner Mavis Muckle, our next-door neighbour. He unpacked his trunk with a tremendous sneeze!

Mavis popped her head out of the tent. "Och, hello Porridge, are you here with the McFun family?"

I pointed up and up and up and up and up and up and up and up and up at a tall megalosaurus! Mavis looked up and up and up and up and up too. Och, she got such a fright that her hair turned white, but it was white anyway so that was OK. Her knees **KNOCK—KNOCK—KNOCKED** but this was no time for jokes.

I dashed after Dino Dad, who darted into a wood made of wood and hid behind some leaves made of, er, leaves. We could hear Fergus's helicopter coming closer...

"I know you're in there!" shouted Fergus. He tilted the helicopter and fanned the trees until every last leaf had blown away.

Now Dino Dad stuck out like a sore squirrel on a holly bush.

The rusty, gusty rotor blades sent lots of tents flying. A tall blue box suddenly swirled overhead.

"Is that a toilet?" asked Ross.

"Och, aye, the loo," said Mavis, who had just said the best joke in this book.

Fiendish Fergus flew over the bare branches. He could see Dino Dad clearly now. The standing dinosaur was a sitting duck.

# Mmmm. Duck.

"Head for the hills," I yowled (in Dinosaur), pointing to some lumpy bits in the landscape.

Dino Dad thundered towards them, with the pesky helicopter not far behind. Its swinging grabber just missed his head.

# 🐾 Me-phew! 🐾

But it grabbed his flailing tail instead!

# 🐾 Me-boo! 🐾

And all at once, Dino Dad was flipped the wrong way up! I had to do something, so I sprang in the air at su-purr-sonic speed. I landed on his swinging nose and hung from his nostrils like something green and yucky (even though I'm actually green and nice).

Fergus laughed in an *I'm-so-pleased-with-myself* way and flew fast and low over the deep, wet, cold, wet, mysterious, wet loch. So low that my soggy bahookie was bounce-bounce-bouncing on the surface like a tartan skimming stone.

Dino Dad's nostrils began to twitch. (My furry paws were making them itch.) He sneezed!

# AT-CHOOOO!

And sent me head over eels into the deep, wet, cold, wet, *eel-filled* loch that I told you about earlier.

Was this the end of the incredibly funny, brave, handsome, clever, good-at-coming-up-with-adjectives Porridge?

 **Me-????**

Was this the end of the incredibly funny *Porridge the Tartan Cat* series (available in all good children's bookshops and all good children's stockings on Christmas Day)?

*Turn the page to find out.*

# 7

# Soggy Porridge

No, of course it wasn't the end.

But it was very wet!

## 🐾 Me-SPLOSH! 🐾

I bobbed up and began to swim in circles... and hexagons... doing the duggy paddle, which was *very embarrassing*.

"Porridge needs saving," cried Isla.

"And swimming lessons," said Ross.

The twins ran to a rowing boat, ready to rescue their favourite tartan cat. But before they could start rowing, I mysteriously rose from the mysterious loch on a mysterious hump AND IT WAS ALL A BIG MYSTERY!

Er, until Isla shouted, "Look! It's Nessie! And Nessie has saved Porridge!"

...and the mystery was solved.

To my amazement, I found myself perched on a sleek black hump behind a smiling monster with a long slender neck.

## 🐾 Me-wow! 🐾

It really was...

# NESSIE!

The Loch Ness Monster was an incredible sight. *So* incredible that books would be written about her one day. In fact, one has. This one. *And it's incredible too.*

"The Loch Ness Monster really exists!" whooped Ross.

"I guess rotten old Fergus was right!" gasped Isla, watching the graceful creature glide through the water. "Only, he's caught the wrong monster."

Friendly Nessie swam off through the water at 1000 smiles an hour, which is very fast (and very smiley too). She slowed by a rocky cliff with a wide waterfall gushing over the top. Nessie picked up speed and ploughed into the tumbling wall of wet.

# Me-help!

I was sure I would get **SPLATTED** against the cliff or **SPLIDGED** or **ANY OTHER SQUELCHY WORD YOU CAN THINK OF** except I didn't.

I just got, um, WET.

# Me-drip

Nessie sploshed through the waterfall straight into her hidden home. We were in a secret cave!

So secret only you, me and Nessie know about it. *Quick, make sure no one is reading this over your shoulder.*

# Me-wow wow wow wow wo

My voice echoed all about, and I sounded like a daft dug. (How embarrassing!)

My voice was interrupted when my empty tartan tum grumbled. I wailed, "I'm so hungry I could eat a seahorse."

Nessie wailed too and dipped her head in the inky water. She fished out a fish and flicked it my way.

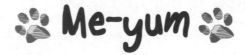

Whenever I wailed, Nessie wailed back and flicked me another fishy treat. After thirty-three trout, I had no doubt that we understood each other.

"Wwwhy wwwere you in the wwwater?" she wailed.

I told her all about fiendish Fergus: how he had captured Dino Dad instead of her, plus his pesky plan to take over the world and destroy volcanoes and fishy biscuits and elephants.

"Wwweee mussst ssstop Fergusss and sssave Dino Dad!" wailed Nessie.

##  Me-cool

Now Nessie and I had a pesky plan of our own!

If only the McFun twins were here to help too.

*If only...*

# 8

# Behind The Waterfall

I glanced up as two children burst through the wall of rushing water. They stood on a ledge at the edge of the cave and waved at me through a swirling mist.

*Ross and Isla!*

The twins gazed around the cavern with 20% surprise and 80% delight, because they had done percentages at school.

I watched them point excitedly at three incredible things:

1. Me

2. My reflection

3. Nessie

"Hi, Porridge! We were four-fifths sure that Nessie and you were behind the waterfall," said Isla, who had done fractions as well.

"We're glad you're OK, Porridge," shouted Ross.

#  Me-too!

I waved at them with my tartan tail.

"I'm glad we don't have a fear of heights," said Isla, as they ran along the high ledge.

"Or weights," said Ross, as they lifted a heavy rock out of their way.

Ross and Isla scrambled down to the rippling pool. The bravest boy and girl you could ever hope to meet or send an email to.

"We need to get Dino Dad back," said Ross, his voice dropping to a whisper. "Do you think Fergus would swap him for Nessie?"

"He might just keep both beasties," sighed Isla.

"Maybe Nessie knows a way to get to him quickly?" mused Ross.

"A way to the sea!" cried Isla. "Let's ask her!"

"Can you help us reach the sea, Nessie?" shouted Isla. "We need to find Fergus's secret secret ship."

Nessie looked as blank as the

spaces        between        these        words.

##  Me-sigh

So I wailed Isla's question and Nessie straightened her long neck and beamed at Ross and Isla like a happy lighthouse. Then she curled her tail around the twins and sat them behind me on two shiny humps.

"Nice one, Ross," said Isla. "Nessie understood you."

*Ahem. It was me!*

Nessie swam off at an unbelievable speed, even though it was true. We hurtled into the darkest part of the cave, clinging to her humps like chewing gum on a school chair.

"This is the Most Amazing Trip Ever!" yelled Ross.

Soooooooo amazing that his teacher would *never* believe him, and he would have to write about something else amazing. *Me!*

The craggy cave became low and narrow as Nessie flew along like a glistening arrow. We journeyed through an incredibly long, dull and boring tunnel that went on and on and on and on and on and on and on and on and on and on and on and on and on and on just like this incredibly long, dull and boring sentence.

It was so boring, I turned over for a nap, just like you turned over that last page.

🐾 **Me-yawn!** 🐾

# 9

# The Incredible Green Hulk

When I woke again, two minutes later, we were still in the tedious tunnel.

## 🐾 Me-sigh 🐾

The gloomy journey was making me gloomy too.

"Cheer up, Porridge," said Isla brightly. "There's always light at the end of the tunnel."

*And she was right!* My *mega-super-well-OK-not-bad* eyes spied a dazzling blue glow in the darkness.

"It looks like a blue moon," said Ross.

(But it wasn't, because you only see those once in a blue moon.)

"It's the deep blue sea," said Isla, who was wise in the ways of seas – especially deep blue ones.

The round exit grew bigger as Nessie swam closer. Now we saw waves and seagulls and waving seagulls.

## *Mmmm. Seagulls.*

Nessie slowed sharply and bobbed into the sunlight.

"We knew you'd know the way." Isla gave her new pal a happy hug.

"Now to find that secret secret ship," said Ross.

We drifted around a quiet bay and stopped in the shadow of a steep brown cliff. My whiskers tingled.

Something about it wasn't right. For a start, it was made of rusty metal. And there were big wonky letters scratched at the top.

FLOATY McFUNGUS FACE

## 🐾 Me-gulp! 🐾

I waggled ma paws at the secret secret ship's name. Isla was the first to look up.

"FLOATY McFUNGUS FACE!" she gasped.

"That's a funny name for a big cliff," said Ross.

"It's not a cliff, it's a massive steam-powered paddle ship," said Isla. "Look: here's a rusty anchor. And there's a wonky paddle wheel."

It was a ship that could only be the secret secret hideaway of He Who Must Not Be Named.

(Him With The Helicopter!)

(What's His Name?)

# FERGUS MCFUNGUS!

## 🐾 Me-oops 🐾

*I said his name.*

"I wonder what's up on the main deck?" said Ross.

I asked Nessie nicely to give us a lift. She lowered her long neck and we all climbed on. As soon as she straightened up, we had a braw view of the ship's main deck. Here's what we saw:

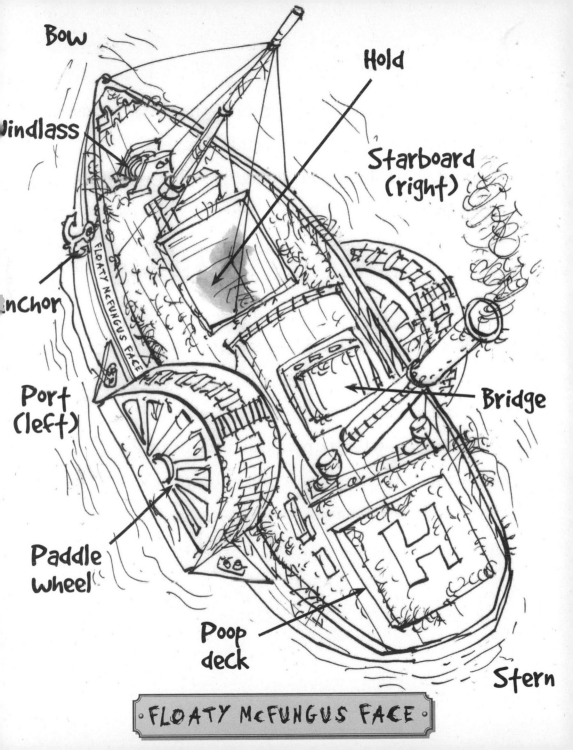

Bow

Windlass

Anchor

Port
(left)

Paddle
wheel

Poop
deck

Hold

Starboard
(right)

Bridge

Stern

FLOATY McFUNGUS FACE

The deck of the paddle steamer was an overgrown mess of moss and mushrooms, held together with rusty nails and lumpy tar from Big Jock's Rusty Nail and Lumpy Tar Emporium. It was a vast vessel as long as a football pitch, and as high as that balloon you accidentally let go of once.

"What's our plan?" whispered Ross.

"We Climb On Board, Rescue Dino Dad and Escape."

It was ever-so-nearly-almost a purr-fect plan. Only Isla forgot to add "And Then Celebrate by Munching a Big Box of Fishy Biscuits".

Suddenly Fergus's helicopter (dangling Dino Dad) clattered into sight and

scattered birds and words all over the place.

Nessie nestled behind a wonky paddle wheel, safely hidden by STINKY strands of seaweed. The awful rotting smell was enough to make the twins' eyes water and my nose water and probably the water below us water. What a whiff. No one would ever sniff us out here.

##  Me-pong

My *mega-super-well-OK-not-bad* eyes watched the helicopter dangle Dino Dad over the deck.

Then my *mega-super-well-OK-not-bad* ears heard him shout:

"I'm going to drop you into this big, empty space that holds stuff. I don't know what it's called."

*A hold!*

Och, he needs a wee peek at my handy diagram on page 67!

The grabber let go of Dino Dad and the mighty megalosaurus dropped into the hold.

THUD!

"You'll never get out," crowed Fergus.

Dino Dad roared and clawed the metal walls.

SKLANG·A·KLANG·KLANGGG!

"This hold is claw-proof, jaw-proof, tail-proof, fire-proof, moth-proof and escape-proof! And here's the proof: I've got a certificate."

Fergus leaned out of the helicopter and waggled a crisp packet that looked just like the one from Chapter 5.

##  Me-sigh

# 10

# All Aboard

I don't know why, but baddies in the movies love to tell people what they're going to do next. And baddies in books are just as bad. *Ahem – as Fergus will now demonstrate:*

"Listen here, beastie!" he hollered from the helicopter. "I'm the Actual Proper Captain of this ship because I'm wearing this Actual Proper Captain's Hat. As soon as I land, I'm going to the bridge because that's where the captain, er, plays bridge and shouts orders like, um, 'Shuffle the deck!' When I'm there,

I'll close the hold, scan all the DNA or B or C in your body and make copies of you."

Dino Dad roared.

"That's right: you are actually inside a mighty-mega 3D printer! I'll copy you countless times, and create an army of mighty-mega monsters to take over the world and..."

# CHOP - CHOP - CHOP

His boastful words were drowned out by the sound of the helicopter landing on the poop deck, which sounds rude but isn't really. Poop deck.

Poop deck. Poop deck. Poop deck. Poop deck. Poop deck. Poop deck. Poop deck.

*I'd rather have a litter tray.*

Once all was quiet, we hitched another lift on Nessie's neck, all the way up to the overgrown deck.

I perched on her snout and keeked through the rusty railings.

##  Me-keek

There was Fergus, standing on the ship's bridge: a vast room with an all-round view and an all-round steering wheel. I could see him easily, but he couldn't see me against the green-blue sea, thanks to my tartan coat.

Suddenly Nessie started to snuffle.

"Your tail is tickling Nessie's nose!" hissed Ross.

I lifted it up.

*Too late.* The Loch Ness Monster let out a sneeze

that blew me onto the deck quicker than you can say, 'fishy bisc—'

AT-CHOOOOO!

*Told you.*

"We'd better follow Porridge," sighed Ross, "in case he gets himself in deep water."

"Aye, there's a lot of that about," said Isla. "Let's go."

The twins quickly shinned up Nessie's neck – and by the time you reached the end of this sentence, they were both on deck and by my side.

*Aren't books brilliant?*

"Quick, everyone. Hide behind this windlass," said Ross. "I read somewhere that it winds up the anchor chain."

*Aren't books brilliant?*

We looked up at Fergus, who was picking mushrooms from his ears and eating them because he thought no one was looking.

#  Me-yuck

"It's time I gave out some Actual Proper Orders because I'm wearing this Actual Proper Captain's Hat," said Fergus. First, he ordered a fish supper. Then he gave the order to "Lift Up the Heavy Thingy at the Pointy Front of the Ship."

"Hoist the Anchor at the Bow, you mean," snapped a stern voice from the stern. So stern and scary it made me tremble.

#  Me-tremble

*Who could it be?*

As we hid behind the windlass, we heard two heavy boots clomp towards us. Then even closer came the screech of a rusty lever. At once, the old windlass began to spin around, winding the anchor chain up from the bahookie of the sea.

# CLUNK·A·LUNK·A ·LANK·A·CLANK

Curious as a cat, I took a wee keek at the stern crew member.

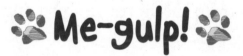 Me-gulp!

A big round windy lass was winding the windlass! *I recognised her at once from another one of my Porridgy adventures. Do you?*

It was...

# 12
# Big Trouble

Give yourself a gold star if you got it right. If you didn't, colour in this one and pretend you did.

The last time I saw Windy Wendy she had gone

and blown off down the street like a leaky balloon.

**floobb-bloobb-flarttle-blurrpp-fflurrpp-frooble-** splib

Now Windy Wendy was before me once more. She was tall as a tenement, and close as a close.

Hmmm, where was I?

I was hiding behind the windlass – beside the twins, who were beside themselves with worry.

"We can't let this ship leave with Dino Dad still on board," said Isla. "Who knows where Fergus will take him."

I had to do something fast, so I wailed down at Nessie through the railings: "Grab the anchor when it comes out of the wwwater!"

## 🐾 Me-wail! 🐾

"What was that!?" cried Windy Wendy. "I heard a big wail!"

"A big whale?" gasped Fergus from the ship's bridge. "Can I grab it?"

"Not a whale, a *wail*," she said. "Made by a *kitty-kitty-kittycat*."

Uh-oh. Those words brought back memories of my time trapped in Windy Wendy's pesky pet shop in *Porridge and the Kittycat Kidnap*.

The twins saw me trembling. "We'll look after you," they whispered, giving me a hug.

"I spy a tartan tail waggling by the windlass!"

 **Me-oops**

I was spotted! (Even though I'm tartan.)

"It's lumpy old Porridge!" sniggered Fergus.

*Charming.*

Windy Wendy took a step closer. I didn't want her

to see the twins so I ever-so-bravely padded into view.

(You've heard of scaredy cats, well this is a *courageous* cat thing.)

"Why is my wee kitty-kitty-kittycat here, I wonder?" She tickled me under the chin with a nibbled fingernail. "You came a long way. Did you miss me?"

"No!" said the twins, springing up like onions. "He's on a mission to rescue our dad!"

"So, we meet again!" Windy Wendy gave the twins

her stern look, even though she was now at the bow. "You twins probably thought you'd seen the last of me, but I'm back like a bad penny – even though ma name's Wendy."

"Wendy McFungus," said Fergus. "My big sister."

_Very big sister!_ I yowled.

Windy Wendy saw the astonished look on the twins' faces. "We're identical triplets," she chuckled. "Identically different."

"But there are only two of you," said Ross.

"You haven't met our brother Fangus McFungus yet," said Windy Wendy. "He's very good at being bad. So be warned!"

 **Me-gulp!**

(I had a funny feeling I would go on a rollercoaster

adventure with Fangus one day – the day the Unfair Funfair came to town – but that's another story.)

The wonky old windlass was still spinning around and s-l-o-w-l-y winding up the anchor chain.

# CLUNK-A-LUNK-A -LANK-A-CLANK

"Don't worry, Porridge," said Windy Wendy. "I'm not interested in tartan cats any more." She pulled a fat rat from her pocket. "A big rat is more loyal than a cat. I call this one Artie."

*Hmmm. I'd have called him 'Lunch'.*

"No more wee pet shops for me," Windy Wendy continued. "I'm going tae build a mammoth zoo."

"Mammoths are extinct," said Ross.

She shrugged. "Nae worries, I'll fill ma zoo with

other big beasties. Starting with the big one in the hold!"

"But that beastie is mine!" Fergus stomped his weedy foot. "I need it tae make an army and destroy the world and do lots of bad stuff!"

Windy Wendy glared at him with big squid-like eyes. Fergus wilted like an old salad leaf left on a school dinner plate.

"OK, I'll give you the original – once I've made lots of copies," he suggested, and she agreed.

"You can't keep the original!" shouted Ross. "That's our dad!"

"That beastie in the hold is *Nessie*," snapped Fergus. "And here's a certificate to prove it."

Once again, he waggled his pesky crisp packet in the breeze. Suddenly it blew off, which sounded rude but wasn't really.

# 13

# Clunk-a-lunk-a-lunk-a-splash

It's lucky you picked up this book today. You're just in time to see a big anchor splash out of the sea:

## CLUNK-A-LUNK-A -LUNK-A- SPLASH!

And watch my pal Nessie clamp it in her mouth!

## 🐾 Me-phew 🐾

Now the pesky paddle steamer was going

nowhere! *Nice one, Nessie!*

I'm full of good ideas.

Wendy was still winding and Nessie held tight:

*The wonky windlass strained in vain,*
*It couldn't wind up the stubborn chain.*
*It shuddered and juddered again and again.*
*And whined and shook like a dug in the rain!*

To sum up: the whole machine was going nuts, especially the nuts.

## 🐾 Me-run! 🐾

Ross hid by the buoy. Then Isla hid by the boy by the buoy. (By the by, I hid by the girl by the boy by the buoy. Oh boy!)

*Just in time.*

# SHUDD-DA-JUDD-DA -BA-BLA-BLAMM!

The wobbling windlass broke into bits! Cogs and
gears flew by my ears.

The long chain rattled loose and snaked along
the shaky deck. Windy Wendy pounced on it like a
mongoose on a rattlesnake. She tied the chain around
her waist and tried to haul the anchor up, all by herself.

"It won't budge!" she bellowed.

She tugged the chain with all her might.

Nessie tugged too and the chain went tight.

*What a sight!*

The two foes battled to and fro.

A wee bit this way.

> A wee bit that way.

A wee bit not moving at all.

> A wee bit that way.

A wee bit this way.

A wee bit not moving at all.

A wee bit this way.

> A wee bit that way.

A wee bit not moving at all.

> A wee bit that way.

A wee bit this way.

A wee bit not moving at all.

*Och, it went on for ages.*

Long enough for you to go to school and write all about a tartan cat, then draw a brilliant picture of a tartan cat and sing lots of songs about a tartan cat and pick up a book about a tartan cat and turn to Chapter 14.

# 14

# Anchor Away

"Don't let the monster get away!" shrieked Fergus. "Pull up that anchor!"

"Nae worries," said Windy Wendy. "I'm really strong."

Aye, she was stronger than Godzilla and Gorgonzola put together. She was

# GORGONZILLA!

*What a cheesy joke.*

Windy Wendy leaned back and pulled the stubborn anchor chain. The ship tilted over and soon had a list. Not a GOOD LIST like one you write to Santa at Christmas. No, a BAD LIST – so bad that if we tilted much more the ship would flip! Och, and I would get wet. And you know I don't like it when I'm a soggy moggy.

By now, poor Nessie was nearly out of the water.

There was lots of wave crashing, flipper splashing, tail thrashing, teeth gnashing *and* camera flashing.

"This is a moment I want to remember!" Fergus said, snappily.

"We need to save Nessie!" yelled Isla.

"And Dino Dad!" shouted Ross.

##  Me-WAIT!

I suddenly thought of a simple way to save them. All I had to do was wail at Nessie to let go of the anchor. And send it flying into the hold. Then Dino Dad could climb up the chain and...

"Porridge, do something!" Isla groaned.

I wailed at Nessie to let go of the chain. She opened her mouth and fell back in the sea with a satisfying

Windy Wendy fell back – onto her bahookie –
and accidentally yanked the anchor over her head.

# WHEEEEE!

*Duuuuck!* I wailed at Dino Dad.

## Mmmm. Duck.

The heavy anchor flew like the worst kite in the world, and crash-landed loudly in the hold...

Just as I'd planned!

## 🐾 Me-phew 🐾

Dino Dad roared with astonishment and delight.

I roared back: *Climb up the chain!*

He had to be quick. We're running out of chapters...

# 15

# Identically Different

While you were turning over the page, Fergus helped Windy Wendy onto her feet. She still had one end of the long chain wrapped around her waist. Could Dino Dad really use it to pull himself up?

*Claws crossed.*

My *mega-super-well-OK-not-bad* ears twitched as six dinosaur claws took hold of the chain. Next they heard Fergus whispering to his sister.

"Let's make Porridge and the twins walk the plank."

"We don't have a plank," his sister hissed back.

"OK, let's **boing** them into the sea with this bendy toadstool," he whispered.

"We can hear you," giggled Isla.

"You really are rubbish at whispering," sighed Ross.

"Prepare to be **boinged**!" Windy Wendy boomed. She straightened herself up to a menacing height. Then stood on her tiptoes to look even more menacing.

## 🐾 Me-shudder 🐾

I was such a scaredy-cat that my tail twanged up and my fur stood on end. *Och, I looked like a tartan toilet brush.*

## 🐾 Me-sigh 🐾

Windy Wendy bounded high off the springy deck, like an astronaut but without the helmet or the space suit, so not really like an astronaut at all.

"In one more bound I'm bound to get you, Porridge!" she whooped.

I was too scared to move. Stuck to the spot like a lump of squished chewing gum.

## 🐾 Me-shiver! 🐾

Windy Wendy whooshed up... but she didn't come down. Instead, she hung in the sky like a tethered balloon. Then she shot back towards the hold.

"Something's pulling the chain!" she yelped, grabbing the ship's funnel to stop herself falling. Her legs were waggling wildly now, and her mouth was opening and closing like a thirsty goldfish.

# Mmmm. Goldfish.

Something in the hold *was* pulling on the chain, climbing up slowly... like a spider from a drain.

I spy with my little eye, something beginning with **D**.

# 16

# Not A Donkey Named Dave

It was Dino Dad!

Each time he hauled himself upwards on the chain, we saw a bit more of the mighty megalosaurus. A head, two claws, a wobbly belly.

*Och, this was better than watching the telly.*

"You can do it, Dino Dad," the twins yelled together. "Just one more tug!"

Dino Dad pulled himself out with

## ONE LAST MIGHTY-MEGA TUG.

"Help! I cannae hold on," cried Windy Wendy. Her fingers flew off the greasy funnel and she plummeted past him as he got to his feet and let go. She hurtled into the hold, trailing the loose chain.

Och, she rattled like keys dropped down a drain.

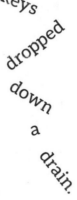

Free at last, Dino Dad curled his tail around the twins and lifted them onto his back. They gave him a hug, and he lifted me too. We got a great view!

"There's no way Windy Wendy can get herself out of there," whooped Ross.

## 🐾 Me-phew 🐾

"I'm trapped!" Windy Wendy sobbed, feeling
sorry for herself. Tears of anger streamed from her
eyes and bogies of annoyance ran from her nose.

#  Me-yuck!

And there, dear reader, Windy Wendy would have stayed forever – or at least until the end of this book – if it hadn't been for Fergus and his pesky helicopter. He took off, hovered high above the hold and lowered the giant grabber.

It pinched Windy Wendy by her coat, and Artie the rat fell from her pocket into the hold. Meanwhile, Fergus lifted his big sister into the sky. She swung in wee circles like a conker. As they flew above the deck, the grabber groaned loudly. Fergus groaned loudly too.

"You're too big to lift!"

"Quick, put me down!" snapped his big sister.

Windy Wendy soon got her wish. Her old coat

ripped where the grabber fingers had gripped.

# RIPP-PIP-PIP-PIPPP!

The coat tore in two.

And
she
fell
feet-first
into
the
funnel.

SHUUUWOPPP

She was wedged like a cork in a bottle.

"Help me, Fergus! I'm wedged like a cork in a bottle."

*Och, I just said that!*

"First, I'll dump this beastie back in the hold," yelled Fergus, swinging the chopper towards Dino Dad.

"Go away!" we all wailed, still on Dino Dad's scaly back!

My *mega-super-well-OK-not-bad* eyes watched Fergus like a hawk.

## Mmmm. Hawk.

He pushed a lever and opened the grabber, ready to snatch us up like that hawk I just told you about...

## 🐾 Me-gulp 🐾

# 17

# Up, Up and a Whiff

Three metal fingers grabbed Dino Dad by the tip of his tail. Once again, he was whisked off his feet – *and we were whisked with him!*

"We need to stop that grabber," shouted Ross.

"How?" yelled Isla.

*Easy. Just climb up to the cockpit and push the lever,* I meowed.

She didn't move.

#  Me-sigh

She doesn't speak Cat.

Before I could stop myself, I had nimbly nipped up Dino Dad's tail. Then I leapt on the grabber and climbed up the chain.

I *love* climbing.

(It's a cat thing.)

"It's a good job Porridge has got nine lives." Ross grinned, as I jumped into the helicopter and squeezed under the seat.

My bahookie bumped against a button.

## Me-oops

It turned the 3D scanner on!

I keeked down just in time to see a light flash over Artie the rat, who was still in the hold. I heard a squeak, then another. Artie had an identical brother! And another! In seconds, the hold was packed with fat, furry rats!

Fergus McFungus didn't notice. He was too busy controlling the grabber and eyeballing the bulging funnel. The funnel was full of steam that couldn't get out, and the pressure was building below his big sister.

**GRUMMMMBBLE-RRRUMMMMBLE**

*Och, the tiniest thing might set it off.* It rumbled like an angry volcano about to blow its top.

Fergus was worried. "Did you have beans today?" he yelled.

"Oh, yes," she said, "just one or two... hundred tins."

"Oh, no," said Fergus.

"Oh, no," said the twins.

"Oh, no," said everyone who has ever read *Porridge the Tartan Cat and the Kittycat Kidnap.*

# 🐾 Me-gulp! 🐾

Beans ALWAYS make Windy Wendy windy.

Just then, there was a tiny – hardly heard it at all
– did it really happen? –

## TRUMP-PA-RUMP!

# 🐾 Me-phew! 🐾

Followed by a thunderous

# TRUMP-PA-RUMP!

*Oh no!*

The funnel started shaking. Windy Wendy began
quaking. (And somewhere in Tattiebogle Town, Groovy
Gran was baking, but that's not important right now.)

Suddenly Windy Wendy blasted up like a rocket, leaving a VERY STINKY trail in the sky!

The rickety ship began falling to bits. As the water gushed into the hold, thousands of identical rats rushed over the edge like rats leaving a sinking ship.

# 18

# Rats

By now, Windy Wendy was whooshing up towards the helicopter.

"Get oot ma way!" she wailed.

# CRASH-BASH!

Windy Wendy walloped the skids off and carried on going. The chopper whirled and swirled out of control.

"Abandon spinny thingy!" shouted Fergus, because he couldn't remember what a helicopter was called.

He coolly stepped out of the cockpit

# AND STOOD IN THE SKY!

## 🐾 Me-how? 🐾

"What a lovely day
to be wearing jet boots,"
he cackled, doing a wee
somersault, just to
show off.

But what goes up must
come down. Which is why
Windy Wendy dropped
like a stone towards a very
gloaty, floaty Fergus.

"I said 'Get oot ma way!'" she bawled.

TOO LATE! Brother and sister bashed together and plummeted into the choppy sea!

**WHEEE-EE-EE-SPLOOOSHH!**

Full of air, Windy Wendy bobbed around sadly, looking blue as a whale. Fergus clung to his soggy sister as if she was a dingy dinghy.

And there we must leave them... as I was busy TRYING TO FLY A HELICOPTER! WITH A DINO DAD AND TWO KIDS HANGING OFF IT! The trouble was, I couldn't reach the pedals. Soon, things got really bad! First a carton of Fergus's mouldy old milk went off. Then lots of NOISY alarms went off too!

# BEEP-BEEP-BEEP-BEEP-BEEP-ETC.

All around me, bells were ringing. Lights were flashing. Now the water was ever-so-very close! In a page or two, this book would get very soggy.

 Me-HELP!

# 19

# Dabble with the Dibble

The chopper hurtled towards the sea. Its flashing
dashboard was lit up like a Christmas tree.

 **Me-gulp!**

Isla scrabbled into the cockpit and sat me on her lap.
"We've come to help," she said. "We could see you were
having a bit of bother so we climbed up the grabber!"

Ross leapt in beside his sister. "Can anyone fly this
thing?"

"Aye!" she yelled. "First, I need to pull back the control stick, then flobble with the flibble and dabble with the dibble."

(Or something like that. It was all a bit compli**CAT**ed for an uncompli**CAT**ed **CAT** like me.)

"I'm glad Porridge got you that computer flying game," said Ross.

*So was I.*

(Mum always gives the twins birthday presents from me. I help her tie them up with string.)

## Mmmm. String.

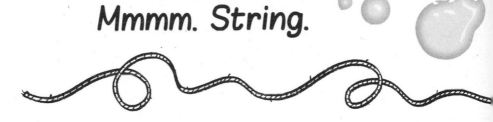

There was a lot of soggy sea not far away. Below us, still grasped by the grabber, Dino Dad was already getting his feet wet!

*Not for long.* Isla cleverly bibbled some wibbles and the chopper swooped up, up and away from the sea!

 **Me-phew**

"I spy Wendy and Fergus," said Isla, pointing down to the soggy siblings.

"Bang goes ma zoo," Windy Wendy grumbled at Fergus. My *mega-super-well-OK-not-bad* ears heard every word.

"Bang goes ma plan to take over the world!" he snapped back. His wet jet shoes were waterlogged so he'd hitched a lift on his squelchy sister. All the ship's rats had the same idea too. They swarmed aboard Windy Wendy and Fergus to dry in the sun.

"Rats!" whooped Windy Wendy, cheering up at last. "This one looks like Artie. And this one. And this one... Och, who needs a zoo? I've got all these big, fat furry cuties to look after now!"

"Rats," grumbled Fergus, as they nibbled his Actual Proper Captain's Hat into Actual Proper bits.

"Porridge, Isla, look!" shouted Ross. "There's Nessie! Thanks for helping us rescue our dad!"

We waved goodbye. Nessie nodded her sleek head and vanished beneath the surface.

"No one will believe that we saw the Loch Ness

Monster," laughed Isla.

"Or that she helped us save our Dino Dad," chuckled Ross. He looked at me. "I think Porridge should get lots of credit."

*I think Porridge should get lots of fishy biscuits,* I meowed.

# 20

# Down In The Mouth

Soon we had left the sea behind. Dino Dad swung gently from the grabber, while mountains and rivers and pigeons flew by.

## Mmmm. Pigeons.

"Not far to go now," said Isla, navigating by a crumpled map. She followed the River Ness as it snaked across a green blanket that wasn't a green blanket at all, just a lovely metaphor. (A metaphor is a word you have to look up in a dictionary because I'm too busy right now to tell you what it means.)

Dino Dad was busy too, dodging tall trees and high rooftops, and roaring with delight.

"Anyone who looks up will get a shock," said Ross, and he was right.

Dud McPud looked out through his bedroom window and got a shock. (Then he got a sock because he was getting dressed.)

A mysterious stretch of water appeared before us and it kept on being mysterious until I saw a sign saying:

and then it wasn't mysterious any more.

"Can you land Dino Dad back by the dig?" Ross asked his sister.

"I think so." Isla's hands trembled as she lowered him down, opening the grabber as soon as his feet thudded on the ground.

"Dino Dad's fine," said Ross. "But we're in trouble."

"Aye, it's going to be tricky to land safely," Isla muttered, "Windy Wendy knocked the skids off."

# KRUNCH!

*No problem.*

A mighty-mega mouth snapped shut – Dino Dad had caught the chopper in his choppers! We dangled high above the shore.

 Me-tremble

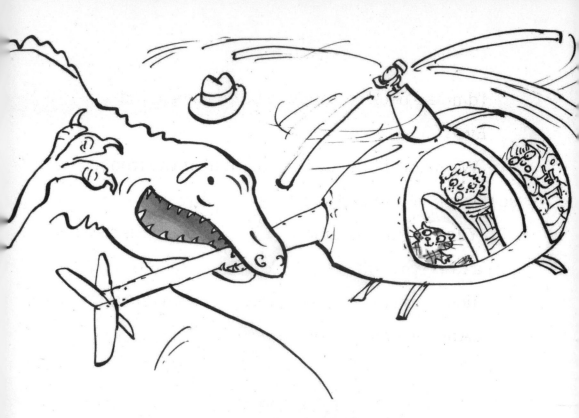

"It's a long way down," Isla said to Ross, seeing the worried look on his cat.

But Dino Dad bent down and gently placed the helicopter by the dig, right next to the broken wishbone. I jumped out to stretch my legs. And kiss the earth and stroke a rock and hug a tree...

I'd never been so happy to be on the ground.

*Ever.*

"We made it!" yelled Isla, turning off the frooble so the zooble stopped spinning.

"Your flying was amazing." Ross hugged his sister like a favourite teddy.

I flopped on the grass because it had been a long day...

...And I'm only a short cat.

## 21

# Gloopy Glue

Ross tickled me under the chin.

 **Me-purr**

"Porridge, you were brilliant," he said, softly.

*Aye, I was.*

The adventure was over. I jumped on the car roof and twanged the aerial, ready to go.

(It's a cat thing.)

"We can't go yet, Porridge," said Isla. "Dad is still Dino Dad."

"We need to change him back," said Ross. "He won't fit in the driver's seat!"

Och, I'd forgotten all about the giant dinosaur next to me.

"We have to think of something fast," said Isla.

I thought of a racing car. But that didn't help.
Then I thought I would build a machine to take us
back in time and stop Dino Dad from snapping the
wishbone! I got to work, scooping up whatever I could
find nearby. Before long, I had made a sandcastle.

"Er, thanks, Porridge," said Isla.

*Och, I'd tried my best.*

I flattened the sandcastle with my bahookie (it's
a fat cat thing) and tried to think of a way to change
Dino Dad back. It was a bit of a puzzle.

#  Me-WAIT! 

Some puzzles need to be put back together!

Dad became Dino Dad when he broke the wishbone apart... Maybe Dino Dad could be Dad again if he put the wishbone back together?

I roared at the big beastie to piece them together.

#  Me-roar! 

Dino Dad agreed to try. He grabbed one half with his tail and licked it like a lolly. It dripped with dino drool.

#  Me-yuck!

Then Dino Dad joined both halves together, and the gloopy drool set like glue.

The twins suddenly realised what Dino Dad was doing.

"Make a wish!" they urged.

I meowed and Dino Dad nodded.

*UrrghwisssshhhurrghwarrrsssDaadddd!* he roared.

And quick as a **FLASH**, Dino Dad became Dad again!

#  Me-phew!

He ran over to the loch and looked at his reflection. He looked like his normal self, maybe an inch or two taller. And perhaps his fingernails were more pointed. It was hard to believe he had been a stomping chomping dinosaur.

"I'm me again," he said, in a daze. "Was I really a mighty megalosaurus?"

"Aye," said the twins.

"And did we really meet Nessie?" spluttered Dad.

"Aye," said the twins.

Still unsure, he stood by the shore, then turned and said softly, "Time to go home, I think. But first, we ought to take this fabuliffic fossil to the museum."

As Dad drove off, I took one last look at the loch through the rear window. All of a sudden, my *mega-super-well-OK-not-bad* eyes saw a big sleek beastie splash out through the waterfall.

# NESSIE!

She saw me too and beamed the most dazzling smile I'd ever seen. I'd draw you a picture but you'd need mega-dark sunglasses to look at it. Then, with a wave of her tail, she was gone.

## 🐾 Me-wow! 🐾

Today I learned two brawsome things:

1) NESSIE IS REALLY REAL...

2) AND WISHES REALLY DO COME TRUE!

*Really really they do.* So in that case, I really really wish:

a) milk was mice-flavoured

b) only pesky dugs got pesky fleas

c) I had a cat flap.

# 22

# Knock Knock

Who's there?

*Ivor.*

Ivor who?

*Ivor newspaper for you.*

Ivor, the delivery boy, cycled away from the house with a grin on his face. I picked up the Tattiebogle Bugle with my tail and carried it into the kitchen, which was full of Big Yins tucking into Mum's experimental sherbert-flavoured sausages and turnip toast.

"I wonder what's on the front page today?" Mum
unfolded the newspaper and everyone took a look.

**TARTAN NESSIE LURKS IN LOCH**

Mum howled with laughter. I howled with
embarrassment when I saw my big bahookie in the
photograph.

It wasn't a cool look at all. *Minus cool.*

"Porridge, you're famous," giggled Ross.

"They thought you were the Loch Ness Monster, Porridge," chuckled Dad. "Unbelievable."

"The twins thought *you* were a dinosaur," said Mum, raising an eyebrow.

"It's true!" said Isla, "Isn't it, Porridge?"

*Aye,* I meowed. To prove it, I jumped on the table and batted Dad's phone out of his bag. Then I switched it on with a swish of my paw.

My **SU-PURR** selfie flashed up on the screen.

*See? I said I'd show you.*

"That's amazing," spluttered Mum.

"I really *was* a mighty megalosaurus!" exclaimed Dad. "My wish came true."

"Told you, Mum!" giggled the twins.

My tartan tum **rumbled**. I padded over

to my empty food bowl, and wished it was full.

Suddenly I saw a magical sight as yummy fishy

biscuits fell from the sky... where Mum's hand was

tipping a box.

*Purr*-fect!

"Now Porridge's wish has come true too," laughed Mum.

## 🐾 Me-yum! 🐾

# I LOVE FISHY BISCUITS!

# CAT ~~ACTIVITIES~~

There are ten differences between these two pictures. Can you spot them all?